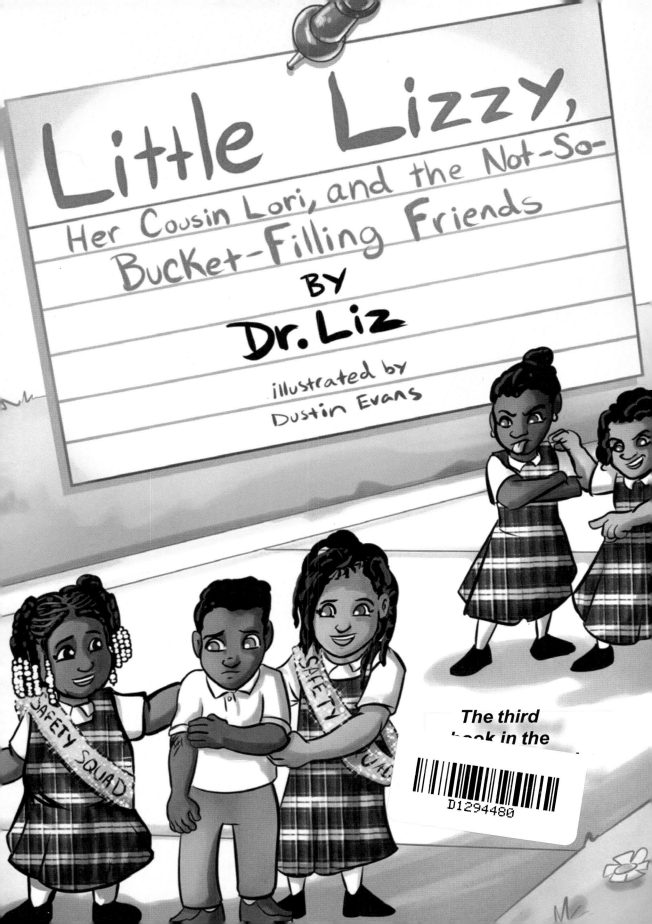

Little Lizzy, Her Cousin Lori, and the Not-So-Bucket-Filling Friends

By Dr. Liz
Illustrated by Dustin Evans

Printed in the United States of America
Perfection Press

ISBN Paperback: 978-1-62920-980-7
ISBN Hardcover: 978-1-0878-9082-1

Visit Little Lizzy online at:
www.littlelizzy.org

This book is dedicated to my nieces and nephews. Thank you for allowing me to practice my bucket-filling lessons on you. Being my first students helped me create the very first bucket-filling school in NYC.

—Dr. Liz

Summer was coming to an end. Little Lizzy was so excited to go back to school.

But Little Lizzy wasn't so little anymore. She had grown a lot over the summer. She no longer fit into her school uniform— or anything else, for that matter.

Lizzy and her family spent the next week getting ready for the new school year. They bought school supplies, new book bags, and shoes.

Lizzy's mom also took her to Ideals Department Store to buy new uniforms. There, the store assistant measured Little Lizzy. She had gone up two uniform sizes! "That means there's more of you to love," Lizzy's mom said.

Lizzy still felt uneasy about being bigger because all her friends were skinny.

On the first day of school, Lizzy was up early. She got ready in a flash. Lizzy ran to her cousin Lori's house so they could walk to school together. Lori and Lizzy were the same age. They had always been in the same class since pre-kindergarten.

Lori and Lizzy talked about all the things they hoped to do during the school year. Lori wanted to join the cheerleading club. Lizzy wanted to be a teacher's assistant at lunchtime. She loved reading to the younger kids.

They both hoped the trouble girls would not be returning to school. Lizzy was especially nervous. She didn't want the trouble girls to notice her weight gain and make fun of her.

Everyone lined up in the schoolyard. Lizzy and Lori were first in line. Lizzy frowned when she saw the trouble girls walk into the yard.

Lizzy and Lori were seated on opposite sides of the classroom. They both had been seated next to one of the trouble girls.

Going to school was suddenly less exciting. Lizzy made excuses not to go to school. She begged her mom to let her stay home. But Lizzy's mom would not allow it. She made Lizzy go. She made sure Lizzy and her two siblings had perfect attendance every year. She posted the certificates on a wall in the hallway.

One day, there was an envelope on Lizzy's desk. She opened it. Inside was a picture of a hamburger and French fries. They had legs and faces. Lizzy was the round burger. Lori was the skinny fries.

Lizzy put the picture in her pocket. She took the bathroom pass and signed herself out of the classroom. She was gone for so long that the teacher sent Lori to find her.

Lori found Lizzy crying in the bathroom. Lizzy told her about the drawing. Lori was skinny. Lizzy wanted to be skinny, too. Lori hugged her cousin. "The trouble girls are jealous because we are smart and beautiful. And they don't have cousins to be their best friends," Lori said.

Lizzy got through September somehow.

Lizzy never told anyone what was going on in school. Only Lori knew how challenging school had become. In October, the teachers announced that it was Anti-Bullying Month. There would be a special assembly. Lizzy hoped the trouble girls would learn something.

The day of the assembly arrived. Everyone was allowed to wear orange for Anti-Bullying Awareness Day. The principal introduced the guest, Carol McCloud. She was an author. She read her book out loud. It was called *Have You Filled a Bucket Today?*

Ms. McCloud told the children that everyone has an invisible bucket. It holds our good thoughts and feelings. Kind words and actions fill the bucket of the person you help. They also fill your own bucket. It is a win-win. Everyone is happy from the good deeds. She said that sometimes, people say mean or hurtful things that dip into your bucket and steal your happiness. Putting an imaginary lid on your bucket helps you keep your happiness.

Ms. McCloud had everyone stand up and face a partner to practice saying kind things to fill someone's bucket. Then, everyone discussed how it made them feel.

The principal also spoke. He said that it was okay to tell someone who is bullying you how they were hurting your feelings. He said to put up your hand and say "Stop!" as loud as you can.

Lori and Lizzy looked at each other. After the assembly, they decided they were going to put a lid on their bucket whenever the trouble girls said mean things to them.

The next day, Lizzy and Lori were playing a game of jacks together. The trouble girls came over. They kicked the game pieces. Everything went flying. "Hamburger is too fat to pick them up," the trouble girls laughed. "Maybe French Fry should do it."

Little Lizzy said, "Stop! Our sizes don't matter. It doesn't take away from who we are. But you're being very ugly." The trouble girls were shocked. No one had ever stood up to them before. Lizzy and Lori high-fived each other. Then, they walked away.

From that day on, the cousins always stood up for themselves. They wouldn't let the trouble girls dip into their buckets anymore. They used their words and their lids wisely.

Lizzy and Lori formed a school safety squad. They helped all the kids at recess feel welcome. They even wore safety squad sashes that they made themselves. They spoke up when they saw someone being bullied. Soon, others joined them.

The trouble girls suddenly found themselves alone.

Later, Lizzy invited the trouble girls to play double Dutch with her. They agreed. Everyone had fun. At the end of recess, they asked Lizzy why she had invited them. "You looked sad," Lizzy said. The trouble girls began to cry. They apologized for being so mean.

At the end of the school year, there was another assembly. Each student got an award. Some were in math, reading, or art.

Lizzy and Lori waited to see when their names would be called. Finally, the principal got to the last two awards...

"These awards go to two special young ladies," he said. "They are good citizens and good friends. They have taught us all how to be upstanders and not bystanders."

The awards had Lizzy's and Lori's names on them! The girls accepted their awards together. They had learned to do the right thing—and had taught others how to do good, too.

Made in the USA
Middletown, DE
03 March 2023

26103038R00015